Thumbelina

By Hans Christian Andersen
Illustrated by Gustaf Tenggren

P9-BYC-040

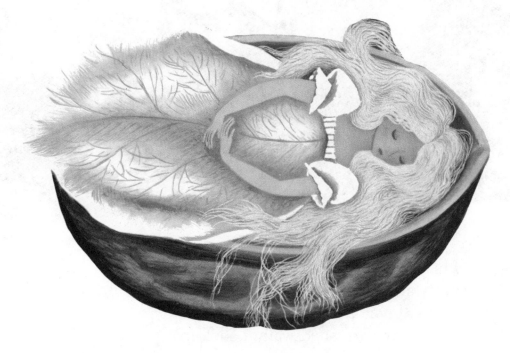

A Golden Book • New York

Western Publishing Company, Inc., Racine, Wisconsin 53404

Copyright © 1953 by Western Publishing Company, Inc. Copyright renewed 1981. All rights reserved. Printed in the U.S.A. No part of this book may be reproduced or copied in any form without written permission from the publisher. GOLDEN®, GOLDEN & DESIGN®, A GOLDEN BOOK®, and A LITTLE GOLDEN BOOK® are trademarks of Western Publishing Company, Inc. ISBN: 0-307-03001-6 / ISBN: 0-307-60149-8 (lib. bdg.)   C D E F G H I J K L M

There was once a tiny little girl. She was sweet and pretty and no taller than your thumb, so Thumbelina was her given name.

A nicely varnished walnut shell made a bed for her, with a violet-petal mattress and a rose-leaf coverlet.

That was where she slept at night. But in the daytime she played about in a small dish garden where she rowed her tulip-petal boat from side to side on a tiny flower-wreathed lake.

It was the most charming sight she made, and she sang as she went in the sweetest little voice you ever heard.

One night as she lay in her pretty bed, a great ugly toad came hopping by and saw the lovely maiden.

"She would make just the wife for my son," thought the toad. So she snatched up Thumbelina, walnut shell and all, and hopped off back to the garden with her.

There, in the muddy bank of a wide brook, the toad made her home with her ugly son. Now, while she decorated a room in their house with rushes and leaves for her daughter-in-law, the mother toad left Thumbelina, in her walnut-shell bed, on a water-lily leaf floating on the brook.

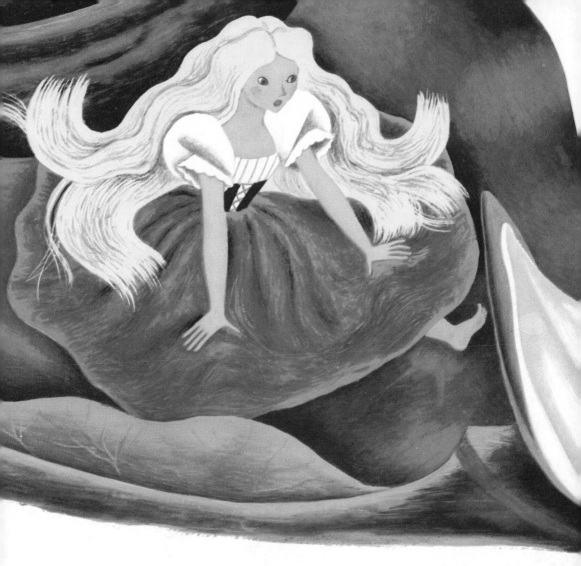

In the morning, when the poor little thing woke up and saw where she was, she cried most bitterly. For the big green leaf had water all around it, so she could not possibly escape.

The little fishes, swimming in the water below, heard her crying. They had caught sight of the ugly mother toad, and they knew what she had in mind. So they all swarmed around the tough green stalk that held Thumbelina's leaf, and they gnawed it through with their teeth. Then the leaf floated, with Thumbelina on it, far down the brook.

At last her leaf boat swirled to a stop against a mossy bank in a strange forest world.

She had no way to travel farther, so all through the summer Thumbelina lived quite alone in that enormous wood. From blades of grass she wove a bed. This she hung neatly under a leaf, where she was sheltered from the rain.

For food she had honey from the flowers; for drink, the morning dew on the leaves. And so she passed the summer and autumn.

Then came winter—the bitter winter. All the birds
flew away. The flowers withered. The great leaf under
which she had lived shriveled to a faded yellow stalk.

As Thumbelina searched for a new shelter it began
to snow, and every snowflake that fell on her was as if
a whole shovelful were thrown on one of us, so
delicate and tiny was she.

On the fringe of the wood she came at last to a field mouse's door. Down below the stubble of a large cornfield the field mouse had a fine snug house, with a whole storeroom full of corn.

"You poor little thing!" said the kindly field mouse when she found Thumbelina shivering at her door. "Come into my warm room and have a bite with me."

The mouse took a liking to Thumbelina at once and invited her to stay for the winter.

"Just so you keep my rooms tidy and nice and tell me stories," she said.

Thumbelina agreed and was comfortable there.

In the evenings the field mouse's neighbor often
came to call. He was a tiresome old mole.

"But his house is even snugger than mine," the
mouse said, "and he wears such a lovely black velvet
coat. If only you could get him for a husband, you'd
be well-off indeed."

Thumbelina paid no attention to this. She had no intention of marrying the mole. He was very learned, she agreed, but he couldn't bear sunshine and flowers and said all sorts of rude things about them, though he had never seen them.

Now, he had dug a long passage from his house to theirs. And there Thumbelina found a bird one day— a swallow, numb with cold and almost dead.

She wove a fine big blanket of hay, and she spread it over the swallow and tucked some cotton wool in at the sides. She brought him water in the petal of a flower and took care of him all winter long.

When she was not caring for the swallow,
Thumbelina spent her time spinning and weaving her
trousseau, with the help of some spiders. For the
tiresome mole had proposed to her, and the mouse
decided they should be married soon.

Poor Thumbelina! She grew sadder and sadder as the wedding day drew near. She would have to say good-bye to the sun and the flowers, since the mole did not care for them.

When spring arrived, bringing her wedding day, and the sun began to warm the earth, Thumbelina opened a hole in the roof of the passage, and the swallow stepped out into the pleasant sunshine.

She watched him with tears in her eyes.

"Come with me, Thumbelina," he begged, for he could not bear to have her marry the mole and live forever underground. "You can sit on my back, and we shall fly away to the warm countries, where it is always summer, with lovely flowers."

"Yes," said Thumbelina of a sudden, "I will come with you." She climbed onto the bird's back, settled her feet on his wings, and tied her sash firmly to his feathers. Then the swallow flew high up into the air, over lakes and forests, high up over the mountains of everlasting snow.

At last they reached the warm countries, where
grapes grew on sunny walls and slopes, and lemons
and oranges ripened in the groves.

The swallow flew on, while the country became
more and more beautiful, until at last they came to an
ancient palace of shining marble, standing among
green trees beside a blue lake. Here the swallow flew
down with Thumbelina.

He placed her on a broad flower petal.

There, in the middle of the flower, was a little man
no bigger than herself. He was the king of the spirits of
the flowers.

"My, how handsome he is!" Thumbelina thought.
And the little king was equally enchanted at the sight
of her. He took the crown from his own head and
placed it on hers. Then he asked her what her name
might be and if she would be his wife.

   She knew at once that he was the husband for her,
so she said yes to the king. Then from every flower
round about a tiny lady or gentleman appeared. Each
of them brought a gift for the new queen, but her
favorite of all was a pair of beautiful wings from a
white butterfly. These they fastened to her back, so
that she could flit with the others from flower to
flower.

Such rejoicing as there was then! And the swallow sat in his nest above and sang for their happiness with all his loving heart.